Dig and Dug
with Daisy
TROUBLE with TRUCKS

Caryn Jenner

Dig, Dug, and Daisy drove off.
Just when they reached the end of the drive,
GRRRRRRR! roared the engine. But the truck wouldn't go.

"Oh no, we're stuck in a ditch!" said Dug.

"And we've got a flat tire!" said Dig.
He picked up a wrench. "I'll fix it."
But they didn't have a spare tire.

"I have an idea," said Dug.

Dug phoned for a tow truck.

"But Uncle Dug, we don't want the fruit towed away," said Daisy.

She opened the gate at the back of the truck. WHOoooMPH! The crates slid out of the truck and into the ditch, followed by the toolbox, a rake, a shovel, and a wheelbarrow.

"Oh dear!" said Daisy.

"Come on," said Dig.
He put a crate into
the wheelbarrow and started
off down the road.
"I'm taking these to
Mrs. Green's store."

"I have a
better idea,"
said
Dug.

Dug arrived with a forklift.
Dig and Dug began stacking the crates.
"Uncle Dug, don't stack the crates too high," warned Daisy.

It was too late. CCRRRAAASH!!!
Down came the crates, scattering fruit everywhere.

"Oh dear," said Dig. He began to rake up the fruit.

"I have a better idea," said Dug.

Dug arrived with a bulldozer.

 SCCCRRRAPE went the bulldozer blade as it pushed the fruit into a big pile.

"We'll need to scoop up all of this fruit now," said Daisy. "I'll do it," said Dig. He picked up some fruit with the shovel.

"I have a better idea," said Dug.